Ash, Kiawe, Mallow, Sophocles,
Professor Kukui, and their Pokémon all
wore golden wigs.

They wanted to look like band members
Alolan Dugtrio and DJ Leo.

Boom, boom, boom!
Fireworks lit up the stage.
Fans cheered as DJ Leo started to spin.
"Alola, yo!" DJ Leo said. "It's showtime!"

"Dug dug dug, TRIO!"
Dugtrio sang to a poppy beat.
Ash and his Pokémon danced along.

After the show, Ash and his friends walked home.

"That was fun!" Ash said.

"*Pi. Ka. Chu!*"

"*Ruff, ruff!*"

Pikachu and Rockruff were big fans!

Suddenly, a Diglett grabbed Rotom Dex's wig and raced away.

"Wig-napper!" Rotom Dex screamed.

Rockruff chased Diglett.

"Hey, yo! Bad news!" said a voice. "This place is private property!"

"DJ Leo?" Ash and his friends gasped.
They had found the band's house!
"Come on in!" DJ Leo said.

Ash was starstruck.

Dug-Leo put on a private show just for Ash and his friends!

"This is so cool!" said Sophocles.

But there was a party crasher!

"Hey, that's the Diglett who stole my wig!"
shouted Rotom Dex.
Diglett popped into the room and started singing.
"Dig, dig, dig. Dig, diiig."
Its voice was amazing!

"*Dig, dig, dig, triooo!*" Diglett and Dugtrio all sang.
"Wow, thank you for a great night!" said Ash.

After Ash and his friends left, Diglett stayed to sing a few more songs.

But Dugtrio was jealous. It wanted to be the star.

"Hey, now," said DJ Leo. "What's up with you?"

Team Rocket saw their chance.

"A battle for the spotlight, eh?" said James.

"Let's go catch Dugtrio!" said Jessie.

Jessie, James, and Meowth put on disguises.
Then they went to meet Dugtrio.

"I'm DJ Bling Charm, yo," said Meowth. "And
you've got talent."

Team Rocket promised to make Dugtrio a star.

"Hold the phone!" said DJ Leo.
"We've got a show tomorrow!"
But it was too late.
Team Rocket lured Dugtrio away.
DJ Leo's band had broken up!

The next day, Ash's friends heard the news.
They were upset.
"Let's go find Dugtrio!" said Ash.
"We've got to get the band back together!"

"Pikachu!" Pikachu pumped a paw.

"But how?" Rotom Dex asked.

"I got it!" said Ash. "Get a whiff of this, Rockruff!"

Rockruff sniffed Dugtrio's scarf.

"Now go and track 'em down!" Ash told his Pokémon.

"*Ruff! Ruff!*" Rockruff barked.

It led Ash to an old shack.

Team Rocket had Dugtrio tied up inside!

Meowth was making Dugtrio sing
backup for *his* band.

"Bing time, bling time, yo yo YO!"
Meowth screeched.

The sound hurt Pikachu's ears!

Rockruff growled.

Ash burst through the door.

"Knock it off!" he shouted.

"Now for the best part," said Jessie. "We get
Pikachu and you get zero!"
"Mareanie," called James. "Use Sludge Bomb!"
James's Mareanie spat giant mudballs at Ash.

Rockruff was ready.
It had a Bite that was worse
than its bark!

"Mimikyu!" called Jessie.
"Use Shadow Ball!"

But Pikachu and Ash were a strong team.
"Pikachu, Iron Tail!" Ash called.
Pikachu jumped over Shadow Ball.
It slapped Mimikyu with its glowing tail.

"How dare you pop the charms off our plot?" asked Jessie. "Mimikyu, stifle them!"
"Mareanie!" James called. "Join in the fun!"
But Team Rocket was in for a surprise.

Diglett had set Dugtrio free!
Dugtrio blocked Team Rocket with
Tangling Hair.

"Awesome!" shouted Ash.

"Quick!" yelled DJ Leo. "Let's wrap this up with Tri Attack!"

"Dug, dug, dug, dug, Trio! Trio! Trio!"
Dugtrio took turns blasting Team Rocket.

And they each had a chance to shine!
Team Rocket groaned as Bewear
carried them away.

"Thank you, Ash and Diglett!" said DJ Leo.
"Trio! Dug, dug, dug, dug!"
The band was back together!
But who would be the lead singer?

"They all get center stage!" said Ash.
That night, Dugtrio took turns singing lead.
And they shared the spotlight with Diglett!

Together, Dig-Dug-Leo were superstars!
And Ash and his friends were in the front
row to enjoy the show.